FINALLY MANDIE LOOKED ahead and saw the chimney of the old house. Smoke was coming out of it! Somebody had to be inside. Looking about for a hidden observation place, she ran behind the old barn and huddled against it. Then she peeked around the corner and stared at the back of the house through thick, overgrown bushes.

"Somebody has to be living there," she muttered as a gust of wind made loose boards in the barn bang. What if the entire building collapsed?

Darting across the yard as fast as the wind permitted, she stopped at the back corner of the house and peered through the window. The curtain was too thick, though, and blocked her view. She tried to listen to find out if anyone was moving about in there, but the wind howled and deafened her, and she was beginning to shiver in the cold.

Mandie was about to leave when she saw the curtain move . . . and a hand straightened the folds. . . .

Don't miss any of Mandie Shaw's
page-turning mysteries!

And look for the next book,
coming soon!

The New Girl

Lois Gladys Leppard

BANTAM BOOKS

NEW YORK · TORONTO · LONDON · SYDNEY · AUCKLAND

RL 2.6, ages 7–10
THE NEW GIRL
A Bantam Skylark Book / July 1999

A Young Mandie Mystery™ is a trademark of Lois Gladys Leppard.

Skylark Books is a registered trademark of Bantam Books, a division
of Random House, Inc. Registered in U.S. Patent and Trademark
Office and in other countries.

Published simultaneously in the United States and Canada.

Bantam Books are published by Bantam Books, a division
of Random House, Inc. Its trademark, consisting of the words
"Bantam Books" and the portrayal of a rooster,
is Registered in U.S. Patent and Trademark Office
and in other countries. Marca Registrada.
Bantam Books, 1540 Broadway, New York, New York 10036.

ISBN 0-553-48660-8

PRINTED IN THE UNITED STATES OF AMERICA

OPM 10 9 8 7 6 5 4 3 2 1

For
Wendy S. Loggia,
great editor, dear friend,
who started Young Mandie on her way

1
Upset Plans

MANDIE SHAW RAN up the pathway to meet Joe Woodard, where he waited for her on the main road. She wanted to ask him something, and she was in a hurry.

"Where's your sister?" Joe asked. He took her books and they started walking down the road toward the schoolhouse. The November wind was strong and cold.

"Irene has a sore throat and Mama told her she'd better stay home today," Mandie replied. Looking up at the tall boy, she added, "So since she won't be with us today, why don't we detour by the old Conley place after school and see if someone has moved in?" Not too long ago Joe had noticed smoke coming out of the house's chimney. Mandie had been itching to investigate ever since.

"That's too far out of the way, Mandie," Joe told her. "It would take so long we'd be awfully late getting home from school, and I know my mother has some things she wants me to do this afternoon."

"Oh, Joe!" Mandie exclaimed, stomping her feet as she walked. "We could hurry. It wouldn't take but a few extra minutes. Please." She looked at him with pleading blue eyes.

"Not today, Mandie, not today. I have to hurry home," Joe insisted. "Not only that, it's awfully cold today and it looks like it might rain. The first nice day we'll go by there."

Mandie had a sudden idea. "Maybe we could go investigate on Saturday," she suggested. "Irene has been running off every Saturday lately and leaving me to do all the work, sweeping the yard and everything. I could just go and leave her to do it all this Saturday."

"Irene may not be well by then. After all, this is Wednesday, you know," Joe reminded her.

"I'll let you know Friday how she is," Mandie said.

"All right, but I'm not promising right now, because I don't know what chores I'll have to do

Saturday," Joe replied. He looked down at her with a big grin. "You know, Mandie, you are a very insistent person when there's something you want."

Mandie grinned back, her eyes crinkling. "I know," she admitted. "That's the only way I can get what I want sometimes."

Joe reached down to tweak the long blond plait of hair that hung below the back of her bonnet. "I'll remember that," he said.

"I wonder why everyone calls that house the old Conley place," Mandie said as they walked on. "I don't remember anybody ever living there, do you?"

"Vaguely," Joe said. "There was an old man who lived there alone. I remember my father saying he had been doctoring the man."

"Whatever happened to him?" Mandie asked.

"I believe he went off somewhere and never did come back," Joe said thoughtfully. "I suppose his name was Conley."

"If you saw smoke coming out of the chimney, maybe he has come back," Mandie said.

"Maybe, but he has been gone a long time, since before I ever started school, and he was real old then," Joe replied as they left the main road and walked down the pathway to the one-room log schoolhouse.

"But you just turned twelve the first of this month," Mandie said as they stepped up on the front porch of the building.

"And I've been going to school six years, so that was a long time ago," Joe said.

They went inside and took their seats as one of the older students began ringing the bell.

Mandie thought about the old Conley house for the rest of the day. Had old Mr. Conley come back?

When Mandie met Joe on Friday morning, she could hardly wait to see if he would be able to go with her to see the house.

"Well, are we going to look at the Conley house tomorrow?" she asked as Joe took her books.

"I'm sorry, Mandie, but I have things to do for my mother that will take up the whole day tomorrow," Joe told her as they walked down the road.

"What a disappointment!" Mandie said with a

big sigh. "I had hoped you'd have enough time to just run by the old house. It wouldn't take long."

"Sorry, but it's impossible," Joe answered. He looked down at her. "How is your sister? Is she coming to school today?"

Mandie shrugged. "I think she's all right now, but she managed to talk Mama into letting her stay home again today."

"Then you'll have to do all the chores tomorrow and you won't have time to visit the Conley place anyway," Joe reminded her.

Mandie shook her head. "Irene is well enough to do her share, and if she tries disappearing tomorrow to get out of any work, why, I'll just disappear too."

"And you might get in trouble with your mother," Joe told her.

"Irene does it all the time and gets away with it, so I'll just do the same thing," Mandie said with a frown.

"And what are you going to do when your mother gets madder than all get-out?" Joe asked.

Mandie took longer steps to keep up with the tall boy as they approached the schoolhouse. She thought for a moment, then replied, "I'll cross that bridge when and if I get to it."

"I'd say you'd better get prepared," Joe said.

As usual, they were the last pupils to arrive. They were never late, but they usually had to scramble to their seats as the bell was rung outside.

"I'm prepared. I'll just tell on Irene for always leaving me all the work to do," Mandie whispered as she rushed to her desk and sat down.

Mr. Tallant, the schoolmaster, called out the day's assignments. The students were divided into four groups, based on their ages. Mandie sighed when she heard that her group would be having an arithmetic test. She knew it was time for one, but today she didn't want to concentrate on anything. All she could think about was when and how she would ever be able to investigate the old Conley place.

Irene and I will have a lot to do tomorrow, she thought as Mr. Tallant passed out a list of arithmetic problems. *We always have to sweep the yard and straighten up the smokehouse, or I should say, I always have to do it while Irene runs away somewhere.*

She was deep in thought and ignoring the sheet of paper on her desk when Mr. Tallant's voice broke through. "You are being timed now. So get to work," he was telling her group. She looked up and found his gaze on her.

"Yes, sir," she muttered, and quickly began reading the first problem on the test sheet.

She had worked out the answer to number one and was reading number two when a sudden idea came to her. Why couldn't she just run off the next day the way Irene always did and go over to the old Conley place by herself? If she cut through the fields it wouldn't be all that far. It wouldn't take long, and she would probably not even be missed!

"That's exactly what I'll do," she muttered under her breath.

Mr. Tallant walked by her desk. "Did you say something, Amanda?"

She looked up at him. "Oh, no, sir. I mean, I was just talking to myself, that's all."

"Do you have a problem with any of the arithmetic questions?" he asked, bending over and speaking softly in order not to disturb the other students.

"No, sir, I don't think so," Mandie whispered. She picked up her pencil and began figuring the sums. Mr. Tallant moved on. If she hurried she could solve all the arithmetic problems and maybe have a few minutes to think about the next day.

She quickly finished the test, folded the sheet of paper in half lengthwise, wrote her name on it, and sat back to look around the room. Joe was busily writing. *He probably has an English test,* she thought. She decided she wouldn't tell him about her plans. He would just try to talk her out of going. But she would tell him all about it on Monday. Mandie smiled. He would be sorry he had not gone with her.

On the way home Mandie didn't mention the Conley house. And when Joe left her at the top of the lane, she raced down to her house to find out what her mother had planned for her and Irene to do the next day.

Mandie eagerly looked around the yard for her kitten, Windy, and Windy's mother, Spot. Mandie had recently solved her first mystery, and keeping Windy had been her reward. There was no sign of them. But when she opened the back door she found them curled up together in the woodbox by the huge iron cookstove. Her mother was cooking what looked like a lot of food.

"Are we having company?" Mandie asked as she began removing her gloves, bonnet, and coat.

"Tomorrow, not today," her mother replied as she checked on a cake in the oven. "Mrs. McGoochin is coming to take her cat home. She figures the kitten is old enough now to be separated from its mother."

Mandie felt a sudden surge of disappointment. If Mrs. McGoochin was coming, she would never be able to go by the old Conley place. As she went around the doorway into the front room to hang up her coat, she asked, "Is the whole family coming, Lucinda and Michael too?" She went back into the kitchen to stoop down and play with the kitten.

"No, just Mr. and Mrs. McGoochin," Mrs. Shaw replied as she stuck a broomstraw into one of the cake layers in the oven to see whether it was done. "The young ones are staying home with their grandmother because it's so cold." She pulled the straw out as Mandie watched.

"It's done in the inside, isn't it?" Mandie

asked as she saw the straw come out clean without any batter clinging to it.

Her mother looked at her and smiled. "That's right. I do believe you are beginning to learn some things about baking." She set the cake layer on top of the stove to cool and bent to remove another layer from the oven.

Mandie smiled back. "Is it going to be a chocolate cake?"

Mrs. Shaw set the second layer on top of the stove to test it. "Of course," she said. "I know very well what is the favorite of all you young people."

"Are the Woodards coming too?" Mandie asked, rubbing Windy's fur.

"All of them for the noon meal tomorrow," her mother said. She stopped to look at Mandie. "Now, I'll have to depend on you to help me. Your sister is still up there in bed with a sore throat."

"Yes, ma'am," Mandie replied with a sinking heart. "Has Irene been in bed all day?"

"Except to come down for a little food at noon," Mrs. Shaw told her as she continued removing and testing the cake layers.

"I'll go see how she is," Mandie said, starting for the ladder on the front room wall. She wanted to see for herself how Irene was.

Her sister was propped up on pillows beneath the heavy quilt on her bed, which stood across the room from Mandie's. She seemed to be asleep, but when Mandie spoke, Irene opened her eyes and frowned.

"Don't bother me. I'm sick," Irene told her in a hoarse voice.

Mandie tried to decide whether she was putting on or was really ill. "I hope you're not too sick to come down tomorrow when the McGoochins and the Woodards come," she told her, watching for her reaction.

"They're coming? Who else? Is anyone else coming?" Irene asked. Now her voice sounded almost normal.

Aha! Mandie thought. *She doesn't really have a sore throat.*

Mandie turned to go back downstairs. "Mama just said Mr. and Mrs. McGoochin and the Woodards, so I don't suppose Tommy Lester and his family are coming," she told her sister. Irene was very interested in Tommy Lester. When he was around she was always disappearing with him.

"That's all right," Irene replied as she pulled the quilt up around her neck. "I'm too sick to go downstairs anyhow."

Mandie stopped to look at her. "I could ask Mama about Tommy if you want me to," she offered.

"Would you?" Irene half sat up.

"I'll let you know in a minute," Mandie promised as she went down the ladder. The room she and Irene shared was much warmer than the downstairs of the house. That was because the heat from the cookstove rose up there. A slight shiver ran over her as she stepped down into the front room and felt the drop in temperature.

She went back to the kitchen. "Are the Lesters coming tomorrow too? Irene wanted to know."

Mrs. Shaw stopped stirring a pot on the stove to look at Mandie. "If Irene is well enough to be asking after that Tommy Lester, then she's well enough to get up and do her share around here. You go back and tell her to get her clothes on and be down here in time for supper and no ifs, ands, or buts about it."

Mandie was surprised at her mother's reaction. "Yes, ma'am, I'll go tell her."

When Mandie went back upstairs Irene eagerly rose up in bed. "Are the Lesters coming?"

"Mama didn't exactly say. But she sent me back to tell you to get your clothes on and come downstairs for supper," Mandie told her.

"I'm too sick to eat," Irene insisted as she curled up again under the quilt.

"I'm only telling you what Mama told me to," Mandie said as she walked back to the ladder. "If I were you I'd hate to have her come up here and get you." She hurried down the ladder.

Irene didn't reply.

Mandie stepped into the kitchen. "I told her, Mama."

"What did she say?" Mrs. Shaw asked. She shoved a baking sheet of biscuits into the oven.

"She said she was too sick to eat." Knowing her mother wouldn't like that answer, she tried to change the subject. "Where is Daddy?"

"You go back one more time and tell Irene if she doesn't get up and get down here I'll come after her," Mrs. Shaw said, lifting the lid from a pot that was about to boil over. "Your daddy's gone over to the Woodards' to get some of that salve from Dr. Woodard to rub on Irene's chest." She frowned. "But now I'm thinking she may not need it."

Mandie didn't like arguments, and she quickly thought of a way to distract her mother. "If you are ready I'll set the table for you now, Mama."

"All right, go ahead," Mrs. Shaw said. "We'll have everything waiting when your daddy gets back. He's worked out there in the cold all day splitting rails for that fence he wants to put around the property. I know he'll be ready to sit down and eat."

As Mandie carefully set the table for supper, she thought about the sudden change in her plans. She certainly wouldn't be able to look at the Conley house the next day, and the day after that was Sunday. Maybe on Monday she could persuade Joe to walk home that way. She just *had* to find out what was going on at the old house! No new faces had appeared in the surrounding countryside, so if someone was living in the Conley place, they had been living there in secret. This was a mystery she had to solve!

2

Goodbye, Spot

MANDIE WOKE EARLY Saturday morning. There was no school, but there was lots of work to be done to get ready for the noon meal. She looked over at Irene, who was still asleep. Mandie decided she would help her mother with the food and let Irene do the sweeping, dusting, and whatever else her mother came up with.

Throwing back the heavy quilt, Mandie got out of bed and quickly dressed. She could smell the aroma of coffee from below. Her father was already up and in the kitchen. She hurried to join him.

As she reached the bottom of the ladder, Spot and Windy came running to meet her. She stooped down to pet them.

"Spot, I'm so sorry you have to go back to Mrs. McGoochin, but then you might be glad to

15

get back home with her after having been stolen," Mandie said, rubbing the mother cat's head. She turned to the yellow kitten. "But, Windy, I got you because of all that. And you're going to have to grow up now and tell your mother goodbye."

Both cats began purring, and when Mandie straightened up, they rubbed around her ankles and almost tripped her as she hurried into the kitchen.

"You're up bright and early," Mr. Shaw said with a big smile. He was pouring a cup of coffee from the pot on the cookstove.

"I smelled the coffee and knew you were up," Mandie told him with a grin. She was nine years old and small for her age, so she had to look way up to her tall father.

At that moment Mandie's mother came into the kitchen. "We need to get started early this morning to get all the cooking finished in time for the noon meal," she said to Mandie.

Mr. Shaw poured another cup of coffee and handed it to his wife.

"I want to help you with the food and let Irene do whatever else you need to have done,

Mama," Mandie said, following her mother to the stove.

"All right, that's fine. Irene can clean up the house and you and I will get the meal ready," Mrs. Shaw agreed. "Is your sister dressed?"

"No, she was still asleep when I came down," Mandie replied. Turning to her father, she said, "I think I would like a little coffee this morning. It's awfully cold."

Mr. Shaw poured a cup for his daughter and handed it to her. "Be careful, now. It's hot."

Mandie held the warm cup with both hands and took a small sip. It really was hot.

"Amanda, go get Irene up. Tell her I said to get downstairs immediately," Mrs. Shaw said.

Mandie quickly set her cup of coffee on the table. "Yes, ma'am," she replied to her mother. "Daddy, I'll be right back if you want me to help you cook breakfast."

"Fine, dear," Mr. Shaw called back to her as she hurried to the ladder in the parlor.

Mandie reached down to shake Irene's shoulder. "Irene, wake up. Mama says to get up and come on downstairs. We're going to eat breakfast in just a little bit," she said to her sister.

Irene jerked away from Mandie's hand, rolled over, and covered her head with the quilt. "Go away," she demanded. "Leave me alone!"

"Irene, Mama sent me up here to wake you," Mandie said again. "And if you don't get up, she's going to be awfully mad. We have the McGoochins and the Woodards coming to eat today, remember?"

Irene threw back the quilt and slowly sat up. "Tell her I'll be down in a minute," she said. "I suppose we'll have to help her finish cooking."

"Oh, no, Irene," Mandie said. "I volunteered to help with the cooking. She said you could clean up the house. The house is not really dirty, so that should be an easy job for you."

Irene looked at her suspiciously. "Then why did you ask to help with the cooking?"

"Because I like to cook. I want to learn how to bake all those pies and cakes and everything that Mama makes," Mandie said.

Irene got out of bed and began putting on her clothes. "Did you ever find out if anyone besides the McGoochins and the Woodards are coming?" she asked.

"No, I don't think anybody else will be here,"

Mandie replied. "Maybe Tommy Lester will come by before then, and you can ask him if his family will be here."

"Now, I didn't mention his name," Irene quickly said, pausing in the middle of buttoning up her dress.

"I know you didn't, but I can read your mind. That's who you were interested in. Tommy," Mandie told her with a big smile. She rushed for the ladder as Irene reached for her.

"I'll get even with you before the day's over," Irene called as Mandie scrambled down the ladder.

After breakfast Mandie helped her mother in the kitchen. She broke up the cake of corn bread her mother had baked so that it could be used to make dressing. She greased pie pans and got another cake of corn bread for the table.

Mr. Shaw had gone to clean up the barn, and Mrs. Shaw had sent Irene to help him. Mandie knew how much work Irene would do—she would disappear the first chance she got.

Everything smelled so good that it was hard to resist the temptation to sample all the delicious food. Mandie did manage to get her finger into the bowl that had held the chocolate icing for the cake layers her mother had baked the day before. She ran her finger around and around inside the empty bowl and licked it.

"Not too much of that, now," Mrs. Shaw told her, looking up from the chocolate icing she was spreading on the cake. "You won't want to eat your dinner if you mess in stuff ahead of time."

"Yes, ma'am," Mandie replied, taking the bowl to the dishpan on the dry sink and putting it to soak.

"Get the plates down from the cupboard," Mrs. Shaw told her. "Let's see, there'll be nine of us."

Mandie counted in her head as she went to get the dishes. "So it will just be the Woodards— Mrs. Woodard, Dr. Woodard, and Joe—and Mr. and Mrs. McGoochin," she said. The Lesters were not coming. That meant Irene would slip out while everyone was there and probably meet Tommy somewhere.

And that was exactly what her sister did. Soon after the company had all arrived later that morning, Irene started for the back door.

"Now, just where are you going?" Mrs. Shaw

asked as she brought platters of food to the table from the stove. Mandie was helping her.

"I was just going out for a minute," Irene replied, pausing with her hand on the door latch.

"No, you're not, not right now. We're a-fixing to sit down and eat," Mrs. Shaw told her. "Amanda, go in the parlor and tell your daddy everything's ready."

Mandie glanced back at Irene, who finally let go of the latch and stepped away from the back door. Then Mandie went into the parlor to give her father her mother's message.

Mrs. Shaw had sent the McGoochins and the Woodards into the parlor while she and Mandie finished preparing the meal. Mandie had not had a chance to speak with Mrs. McGoochin about Spot, or to talk with Joe. And the adults all got busy with their own conversations at the table, so the meal was finished before Mandie had an opportunity to talk to Mrs. McGoochin.

"Mrs. McGoochin, I just wanted to thank you again for letting me keep Spot's kitten," Mandie said, following Mrs. McGoochin into the parlor.

"You are entirely welcome, dear," Mrs. McGoochin said as she sat down. "My children will be so delighted to get Spot back, and we thank you for finding her for us."

"Do you think Windy will cry when you take Spot home?" Mandie asked. She was really worried about separating the baby kitten from her mother.

"She may for a day or two, but you know, this is the only home little Windy has ever had. I'm sure she'll be all right," Mrs. McGoochin replied. "Don't you worry about it."

"Yes, ma'am," Mandie murmured, and turned back to join Joe, who was standing in the doorway to the kitchen.

"Would you be interested in a breath of fresh air?" he asked.

"Sure, just let me get my coat and bonnet," Mandie answered, turning back to the pegs in the parlor where coats and hats were hung.

Joe joined her to get his, and at the same time Dr. Woodard, Mr. McGoochin, and Mandie's father came to get theirs.

"Where are you two going?" Mandie's father asked her and Joe.

"Just around the yard, sir," Joe said. With a glance at his father, he added, "My father always recommends exercise and fresh air after a big meal, you know."

"Just be sure you stay in the habit," Dr. Woodard said, smiling at his son.

"I agree it's a good habit," Mr. Shaw added.

"But it's hard to do on cold days like this one. I can always think up something else to do indoors by a warm fire," Mr. McGoochin added. He was a quiet person who never had much to say.

Mandie and Joe went out the back door, and the men followed. Suddenly Mandie turned to Joe. "Let's ask your father about the man who lived in the old Conley place."

Before Joe could reply, Dr. Woodard said, "There was a man living there at one time, years ago now."

"What was his name, Dr. Woodard?" Mandie asked.

"Well, now, let me see, it was Conley, Miss Amanda. That's why they call it the Conley place," Dr. Woodard explained.

"I remember a man living there. He never wanted to be bothered by visitors, so I never really got to know him," Mr. Shaw put in.

Mr. McGoochin listened, since he had never lived in the area himself.

"What happened to the man, Dr. Woodard?" Mandie asked.

"He went to live with relatives, if I remember correctly," the doctor told her. "And I don't believe he ever came back, so the place just fell apart."

"I saw smoke coming out of the chimney not long ago. Do you think he might have come back?" Joe asked.

"I would hardly think so. He was old, probably in his eighties back then, and in bad health. There must be someone else there now," his father said, walking on down the pathway with Mr. Shaw and Mr. McGoochin.

"I wish we could find out if someone is living there," Mandie said as they started walking around to the front of the house.

"We will, just as soon as we get the chance," Joe promised.

"What about Monday? Do you think we could go by there Monday on our way home from school?" Mandie asked, stopping to look at him.

"I'll have to see if my mother needs me after school Monday," Joe said. "But if she doesn't, then we'll walk home by there."

"Promise?" Mandie asked with a big smile.

"Promise," Joe agreed. "Now, let's get moving before we get icicles."

They walked on around the house, and when they got to the front porch Mandie was amazed to see her sister sitting on the front steps by herself.

"Why are you sitting out here in the cold?" Mandie asked.

Irene jumped up. "None of your business," she said.

"Come walk with us, Irene," Joe invited her.

Irene rolled her eyes. "Walk where? Where are y'all walking to?"

"Oh, nowhere in particular," Joe replied.

"Probably up to the main road and back. Come on, if you want to," Mandie told her sister.

"No, thanks," Irene replied. She quickly walked off in the opposite direction from the one Mandie and Joe had come from.

"Well," Joe said.

"She's headed toward the road up the mountain," Mandie remarked as she watched her sister walking away.

"The road up the mountain? You mean the road to the cemetery? What in the world does she want to go up there for?" Joe asked.

"She was hoping Tommy Lester would come by today, since his family was not invited to dinner," Mandie told him. "Maybe she thinks she'll run into him up that way." She shivered slightly. "Come on. Let's walk up to the road and back."

"Yes, let's do, and let's make it quick," Joe said, patting his gloved hands together as they started on.

"Quick for more than one reason. I know we still have chocolate cake and lots of other goodies. It's all on the table covered up with a tablecloth," Mandie said. She could almost taste the delicious chocolate now.

"Now, who said I was hungry?" Joe teased.

"I know for a fact you are always hungry when there's chocolate cake around," Mandie replied.

They hurried up to the main road and then hurried back to the house. They came into the kitchen through the back door and rushed over to the cookstove to get warm. A fire was kept in the stove all winter for warmth as well as for cooking; the fireplace in the parlor didn't give out as much heat.

Mrs. Shaw came into the room and reached for the coffeepot on the stove. "Get your coats off and we'll have coffee and cake before everyone leaves," she told the two young people.

Mandie saw through the parlor door that her father, Joe's father, and Mr. McGoochin had returned. She and Joe removed their coats and hats and hung them on the pegs. She looked around but didn't see Irene. Either she had not returned or she had gone upstairs.

Everyone had cake and coffee. The Woodards and the McGoochins were preparing to leave when Mandie heard Irene come in the front door. Mandie stepped into the doorway. "Mama has coffee and chocolate cake if you want some."

Irene was removing her coat and hat and hanging them on the pegs. "No, thanks," she said, and quickly climbed the ladder to the attic.

"That's strange, Irene refusing chocolate cake," Mandie said to Joe.

"She'll probably be back down for some later," Joe replied.

But Irene didn't come back down. The Woodards and the McGoochins left, and when suppertime came Irene still had not come downstairs. Mrs. Shaw sent Mandie up to get her, but Irene said she was not hungry and stayed in bed.

"If she's not hungry then I suppose she can stay up there," Mrs. Shaw remarked as she and Mr. Shaw and Mandie sat down at the table.

Irene's probably mad about something, Mandie thought. *I suppose she never did find Tommy Lester.* Even though Irene always seemed uninterested in anything that concerned anyone but herself, Mandie felt sorry for her older sister.

Later that night when Mandie went to bed, she took Windy upstairs with her. Irene appeared to be asleep, but as soon as the kitten began meowing and moving around, she sat up.

"Can't you keep that cat quiet?" she complained.

"I'm sorry, Irene, but I suppose she misses her mother," Mandie said, cuddling the kitten under the covers with her.

"Well, she'd better get used to not having a

mother, because I'm not going to stand for that noise all night," Irene grumbled, and lay back down, pulling the quilt over her head.

Mandie didn't sleep much that night because she had to hush the kitten every time she got comfortable. She too secretly hoped the kitten would get used to not having her mother around.

As she lay there cuddling Windy, Mandie began to think. If Joe couldn't go on Monday, she'd go by the Conley place alone. She wouldn't tell him, though, because he would only try to talk her out of it. But she was determined. She would go Tuesday after he walked her home from school. She would slip off through the fields.

I'll see for myself if someone's living in the Conley place, she thought as she drifted off. *One way or another.*

3

Who's There?

"I'M AFRAID I HAVE some bad news," Joe told Mandie Monday morning. "I—"

Mandie interrupted, "You can't go by the old Conley place today. That's all right." She started walking down the road to school, and Joe followed.

"Not today or tomorrow," he said. "Today—"

"That's all right. You don't have to explain." Mandie frowned and tightened her lips.

"But I do, Mandie," Joe replied, keeping up with her rapid pace. "I have chores to do this afternoon for my mother, and tomorrow my parents will be picking me up from school about an hour early. We have to go into Bryson City on business." He looked down at her as they hurried on.

"Just forget about it," Mandie said, her voice

disappointed in spite of her effort to act as if it didn't matter. "We don't really have to ever go over there."

"But we will, the first afternoon that I have time," Joe insisted. "I'm sorry I've been so busy."

"I'm busy too, so it doesn't matter," Mandie said. She didn't want him to know that it really did.

"Busy? What are you doing?" Joe asked.

"Irene has had a relapse. She's really sick this time," Mandie explained. "I don't know when she'll be able to come back to school, but in the meantime I have to help my mother around the house."

"I'm sorry your sister is sick," Joe said.

"Mama said she probably brought it on herself by running around all over creation Saturday in all that cold weather," Mandie told him.

"Should I ask my father to come and check on her?" Joe asked.

"I don't know," she said. "My mother didn't ask me to give you a message for your father."

"I'll speak to him about her anyway when I go home today," Joe told her.

Since Joe would be leaving early the next day, he wouldn't be walking home with Mandie. She wouldn't have to pretend she was going home and then circle back through the fields to see the old house. She could go there straight from school.

Mandie felt a sudden satisfaction in the fact that she would be on her own. She also felt a little scared when she remembered that her sister wouldn't be there to walk home either. She would really be on her own.

The community at Charley Gap was not large, and the houses were few and far between. The Nantahala Mountains rising up at the edges gave some protection from the wind and cold but also made the days grow shorter and darker in the winter months. By the time school was out each day, the sun had already disappeared behind the mountains.

"Wake up, we're here," Joe said, pulling Mandie's braid.

Mandie suddenly realized they were in front of the schoolhouse. She had been daydreaming. "So I see," she replied.

As they stepped up on the front porch, Joe

touched Mandie's shoulder. "Why did you get so silent? Are you mad at me because I can't go to the Conley place anytime soon?" he asked, his brown eyes worried.

"Oh, no, Joe, I was . . . just . . . thinking about something," Mandie said. She smiled up at him.

"Well, that something must be something awfully serious," he teased.

"Not really," Mandie said, and turned to the front door of the schoolhouse. "Come on. We're going to be late."

"We're early," Joe told her, following her into the schoolroom.

Joe was right. No one was there except Mr. Tallant. He looked up from his desk and greeted them. "I'm glad to see at least two of my sixteen pupils are interested enough in learning to get here early," he said with a smile, pushing back his dark hair.

"But tomorrow I will have to leave an hour early," Joe told him.

And as Joe explained his situation to Mr. Tallant, Mandie wandered back to her desk and began thinking about her plans for Tuesday.

* * *

The next day Mandie woke early and listened to the strong gusts of wind and rain pounding the house.

"Oh, shucks!" she murmured, raising herself up on her elbow to see out the window. The windowpane was completely covered with water, and the view outside was blocked. "Maybe it will quit or at least slow up some by the time school gets out this afternoon."

She looked over at Irene, who was sound asleep. Even if Irene was better today, their mother would never allow her to go out to school in this weather. And unless Dr. Woodard brought Joe by in his buggy to take her to school, which he sometimes did in bad weather when he wasn't out on a sick call, Mandie's father would drive her to school in the wagon and would return for her later. That would really complicate matters. But then maybe she would be able to persuade her father to drive by the old Conley place on their way home. On the other hand, if the rain and wind continued she didn't think he would agree to it.

"Shucks, shucks, shucks!" she kept muttering to herself as she threw back the quilts and hopped out of bed.

She quickly put on her warmest school dress, a navy blue wool with a shawl collar that added warmth. She pulled on her long black stockings and stuck her feet into her high-top buttoned shoes. In the dim morning light she couldn't find the buttonhook that was supposed to be kept on her and her sister's bureau in the corner. Sitting on the floor, she had to button each shoe button with her fingers, which was hard to do with the stiff leather.

At last she was dressed and made her way down the ladder into the room below. When she entered the kitchen she found her father stoking the iron cookstove with more wood before making the coffee. Windy was asleep in the woodbox.

"I'm afraid we've got some mighty bad weather out there this morning," Mr. Shaw greeted Mandie. He straightened, picked up the percolator from the shelf behind the stove, and went to the dry sink to fill it with water from the pail.

"The wind and rain woke me up," Mandie said. "Want me to help you get breakfast ready?" She joined him at the stove.

"Sure," he said with a smile. "But you and I are the only ones who will eat right now. Your mother seems to be a little under the weather. And of course we won't be getting Irene up to go out in all this, with her cold."

"Irene is still asleep," Mandie told him. She went to the cupboard to get the dishes for the meal. "I hope Mama is not getting Irene's cold."

"I hope so too," Mr. Shaw said, pouring flour into a bowl for biscuits. "If Dr. Woodard doesn't come by with Joe to pick you up for school by the time you're ready to leave, I'll get the wagon and we'll go by and pick up Joe. And if all this hasn't stopped by the time you get out of school, I'll be back to get you."

Mandie sighed. She wouldn't explain to her father that she wanted to come home by the old Conley place. She would just wait till school let out and see what the weather was then.

By the time Mandie and her father had finished breakfast, Dr. Woodard and Joe had pulled up in the buggy at the back door. Mandie put on her coat and bonnet, stuck her gloves in her pocket, and hurried outside. Her father followed her to the door.

"Thank you for coming by, Dr. Woodard. I'll pick them up after school if it's still raining," Mr. Shaw called from the doorway as Mandie rushed through the downpour and jumped into the buggy. Joe moved over to let her sit between him and his father—the warmest place.

"I'll be picking Joe up an hour early to go into Bryson City," the doctor called from his seat in the buggy.

"All right, then. Amanda, I'll come and get you if it's still raining. You wait for me if it is," Mr. Shaw yelled above the noise of the rain and wind.

"Yes, sir!" Mandie shouted back as Dr. Woodard turned the buggy to go back up to the road. She brushed raindrops from her coat.

"Sure would have been a good day to stay home and read by a nice warm fire," Joe remarked.

Mandie shivered. "You'd never get through school that way. We have so much bad weather in the winter you would be out half the time." She moved her feet onto the warm stone, next to Joe's. Whoever thought of heating stones in the fireplace to put in the buggy for a foot warmer certainly had been smart. Everyone in the countryside did that in bad weather.

"But I wouldn't want to do it every bad day," Joe said, smiling at her. "Just a day now and then would be enough."

"That could get to be a habit, so I don't think we'd better start that," Dr. Woodard said, holding firmly to the reins as the horse hurried through the stormy weather.

Mandie's mind was already traveling ahead to the time when school let out. Would it still be raining? She was afraid it would be, the way the sky looked. All through the day she kept looking out the window in the schoolhouse. The rain continued pouring down, and when Joe left early it seemed even worse.

Then suddenly, in the middle of her reading lesson, a spot of sunshine fell through the window onto her book. She looked outside. It had cleared! She wouldn't have to wait for her father to take her home. She would rush out that door and head across the fields of dead cornstalks to the old Conley place!

When the bell rang Mandie was the first one out the door, buttoning her coat as she went. Mr. Tallant had not assigned any homework, and she had left her books in her desk. The cold air hit her with a blast of wind. Without taking time to shiver, she rushed on.

A short way up the road she headed into the deserted fields. The dirt was mushy, and her feet stuck in the globs of mud, slowing her down. The wind blew against her so hard, it was all she could do to walk, but she kept right on. She was determined she was going by the old Conley place.

"Squish, squish, squish!" she muttered under her breath as she tried unsuccessfully to dodge the mud puddles. The field was full of them. The hem of her long skirt was dragging in spite of her attempt to hold it up and soon became heavy and soggy. It slowed her down, and she became worried about the time it was taking to cross the field. She was going to be awfully late getting home, and her mother was going to be awfully upset with her.

At last Mandie came out on the road on the other side of the field. Even though it was longer that way, she decided to follow the road instead of cutting across another field. She would probably make better time, considering the mud-soaked fields. The wind blew her wet skirt around her legs, making them feel like ice. She bent her head against the gusts and continued, unable to rush anymore.

Finally she looked ahead and saw the chimney of the old house. Smoke was coming out of it! Somebody had to be inside. Looking about for a hidden observation place, she ran behind the old barn and huddled against it. Then she peeked around the corner and stared at the back of the house through thick, overgrown bushes.

One of the posts on the back porch dangled in the wind, making the roof on that corner droop. The flooring had fallen in, and the steps had rotted. The one window she could see at the back was curtained.

"Somebody has to be living in there," she muttered as a gust of wind made loose boards in the barn bang. What if the entire building collapsed?

Darting across the yard as fast as the wind permitted, she stopped at the back corner of the house and peered through the window. The curtain was too thick, though, and blocked her view. She tried to listen to find out if anyone was moving around in there, but the wind howled and deafened her, and she was beginning to shiver in the cold.

Mandie was about to leave when she saw the curtain move . . . and a hand straightened the folds. Yes, someone was inside!

She waited a few minutes longer, but there was no more movement at the window. Finally, realizing how cold she really was, she lifted her long skirt and ran until she was gasping for breath and the cold air burned her nose and throat.

When she finally reached her yard, she ran for the back door and into the kitchen to the heat of the cookstove. Her mother called from the front room. "Amanda, is that you?"

"Yes, ma'am," Mandie replied through chattering teeth.

"Get upstairs and change your clothes," Mrs. Shaw told her.

Mandie stepped into the front room and

looked toward the end that was partitioned off with curtains for her parents' bedroom. "Mama, are you sick?" she asked.

"Just a little headache," her mother replied from the curtained-off room. "I'll get up in time for supper. You get your clothes changed."

"Yes, ma'am," Mandie said.

She found her sister asleep in the loft, and she quickly took off her cold, sodden dress and shoes. She put on an everyday dress and found her old shoes and stockings and put them on. She felt much warmer, but she grabbed an old shawl from a peg and wrapped it around herself for added comfort. Picking up the wet dress and shoes, she took them downstairs and hung them on pegs near the cookstove to dry.

Windy meowed, stretched in the woodbox, and jumped out to come to her. Mandie picked her up and held her. The soft yellow kitten circled around and around and finally settled down in her lap.

"Oh, Windy, we have some new neighbors," Mandie whispered to the kitten. "But who are they? Why do they stay hidden? Do you think they could be outlaws?"

Just then her father came through the back door. "Did you get home all right, dear?" he asked as he removed his coat, hat, and gloves and hung them up.

"I got home, but it sure is cold outside," Mandie replied, deciding she would not tell anyone where she had been.

"I agree," he said, as he came over to check the percolator on the stove. "Oh, dear, you did get wet, didn't you?" he said, noticing her clothes. "I'm sorry. I had to go to the store and didn't realize how late it was until school was out. Everyone had gone when I came by it."

"That's all right, Daddy," Mandie said. She looked up at him and smiled. "But I do believe a cup of coffee would help right now." She set the kitten down and hurried to the cupboard to get cups and saucers, which she carried to the table.

Mr. Shaw brought the coffeepot over and filled the cups. "That's what I'm thinking too," he said. "Is your mother still in bed?"

He sat down at the table, and Mandie joined him.

"Yes, sir, but she said she'd be up in a little

while," Mandie replied, sipping the coffee. It felt awfully warm going down her cold throat.

"Your sister still in bed too?" he asked.

"She was asleep when I went up there a while ago," Mandie replied.

"Since your mother and your sister are both under the weather, what do you say you and I make flapjacks for supper?" Mr. Shaw suggested with a smile. "And if they're able they can join us."

"With homemade molasses and butter! That sounds delicious!" Mandie exclaimed. She loved flapjacks.

While she and her father were preparing supper, Mandie thought about her afternoon's adventure. She wasn't sure she would tell Joe about it. He might scold her for running off by herself in all that wet weather. But one thing was sure. She was going back again to see if she could find out who was living there. Whoever it was had to come outside sometime.

And she would keep watching and waiting until they did.

4

The New Pupil

WEDNESDAY MORNING THE SUN came out and warmed the air. Mandie was grateful for a sunny day after the wet one before. Irene and Mrs. Shaw were both still in bed when Mandie hurriedly put on her bonnet, coat, and gloves after breakfast with her father and rushed up to the main road to meet Joe.

"Should I tell Joe? Should I not?" Mandie repeated over and over to herself as she approached the road and saw Joe. "Should I? Should I not?" She frowned and squinted, trying to make a decision.

"Guess what?" Joe asked as they met. "I'm free this afternoon. We can go by the old Conley place if you want to." They started walking up the road.

Mandie hesitated. "Well—all right." She decided she wouldn't tell Joe she had been there the day before. Maybe they would see someone at the place.

"And we have a nice sunshiny day for our walk over there," Joe said, smiling down at her.

Mandie bit her lip and thought about the day before, with all that wind, rain, and mud. "But we'll have to stay on the road to go there," she told him. "The fields are too muddy to cut across."

"And we don't want to ruin our shoes," Joe agreed.

Mandie looked down at her shoes. She had managed to clean them and dry them overnight by the cookstove. She didn't want to get them in a mess again. She glanced across the fields as they walked down the road. Huge mud puddles were everywhere.

"Is your sister still sick?" Joe asked. "I forgot to tell my father."

"That's all right," Mandie said. "Your father knows about her because Daddy went over to your house to get some salve for her the other day, remember?"

"That's right," Joe said. "He was gone by the

time I got home, but my mother mentioned it." Joe walked faster as they came within sight of the schoolhouse. "Come on, Mandie," he said. "We're almost late." He ran down the trail to the front door, and Mandie followed.

They rushed in, removed their coats, and hurried to their desks. The bell began ringing. As usual, they had just made it on time.

When noontime recess came everyone stayed inside. It was too muddy to go out. Joe brought his lunch over to Mandie's desk and sat with her to eat. They both had ham biscuits. They talked quickly because recess was only thirty minutes long.

"Do you think someone is living in the old Conley place?" Mandie asked between bites.

"There must be somebody in that house if there's a fire inside to make that smoke come out of the chimney," Joe replied, swallowing. "Of course, it could be that someone was just traveling through and was camping out for a night or so. I'm not sure that house is in shape to live in. It looks awfully run-down."

"But even if it is run-down, someone could still be living there, couldn't they?" Mandie asked, remembering the hand. She was sure someone was living there, whether the house was fit or not.

Suddenly Esther Rogan spoke from across the aisle. "Are y'all talking about the old Conley place? That place is haunted. You'd better stay away from there."

Mandie and Joe looked at her in surprise.

"I don't believe in haunted houses," Mandie declared.

"Neither do I," Joe added. "I saw smoke coming out of the chimney over there a while back, so someone must have built a fire inside. I don't believe anybody but a human being could do that."

"You don't have to believe me," Esther said. "I've heard the grown-ups talking about it. My mother says the old man who lived there died in the house. He just disappeared one day and was never seen again."

Mandie frowned. "Didn't anyone go see about him?"

"What for? That man would run you off his property with a shotgun," Esther told them. "He didn't want anything to do with anybody, and nobody wanted anything to do with him."

"Esther, you don't know what you're talking about. It's been years since anyone lived in that house. Besides, you're not old enough to remember that far back," Joe said, finishing his ham biscuit.

"I'm only two years younger than you are, the same age as Mandie," Esther informed him. "I may not remember the man, but my parents do."

"I'm sure my father knew him too," Joe said.

Mr. Tallant stood up at his desk in the front of the room. "Recess is over," he said. "Let's all get back to work."

There was a big scramble as all sixteen pupils returned to their desks. Joe paused to whisper to Mandie, "Let's be the first ones out the door when school lets out."

"I'll be ready," Mandie whispered back.

Mandie thought about what Esther had said. That old house was not haunted. Mandie had seen a real live hand straighten the curtain in the window the day before. She was sure someone was living there.

When the dismissal bell rang, Mandie darted through the crowd and put on her coat and bonnet, stuffing her gloves in her pocket. Joe was right behind her, and together they ran out the front door. Joe grabbed her books to carry with his.

"To stay on a road we'll have to cut off on the next road to the left," he told her.

Mandie was having trouble keeping up with Joe's long legs, but for once she didn't complain. The quicker they could get to the old Conley place, the quicker they could get on home. The sun had almost disappeared over the mountain, and the wind had turned much colder. She pulled up the collar of her coat and put on her gloves as they walked.

Soon the house came into sight. "See that smoke coming out of the chimney?" Joe asked, pointing. "Somebody had to build a fire inside to make that."

Mandie looked at the thick smoke coming out of the chimney. "Yes. Maybe we can find out who's in there. Do you think we ought to go right up and knock on the door?"

"No, Mandie, we·can't do that," Joe replied. "What would we say if someone opened the door? Besides, there might be some unsavory characters in that house. Let's just stop by the barn and watch." He led the way to the barn. They stopped at the same corner Mandie had stood at the day before.

"But, Joe, no one may ever come out of that house. We might stand here all day and not see anyone," she argued.

"Mandie, we have only a few minutes. Then we have to go home," Joe reminded her. "Let's just watch the windows."

Before she stopped to think, Mandie blurted out, "I watched the window yesterday, and I saw someone move the curtain—"

"You came here yesterday?" Joe interrupted. "In all that wind and cold you came all the way over here? By yourself?"

Mandie nodded, realizing she had given herself away. "You couldn't come, so I came on by myself. There *was* someone in there. I saw a hand straighten the curtains," she said.

"Oh, Mandie, you shouldn't have done that," Joe scolded her.

Mandie and Joe stood there a while longer, watching and listening, but there was no sign of anyone and no sound. Evidently whoever was living in the house didn't even have chickens in the yard, or a cow, or a horse. Mandie wondered about all this and secretly thought maybe Joe was right. Outlaws could be in the house.

"Let's go home," Joe told her as he turned back toward the road.

Mandie reluctantly followed, all the time looking back at the house. She would return as soon as she got a chance.

After she went to bed that night Mandie thought about what she would do if she did return to the old house. *If no one comes out of the house next time, I'll march right up to the door and knock! That's what I'll do.*

But as it turned out, she didn't have an opportunity to do that. The next day at school Mr. Tallant had just called the roll when the front door opened. A tall, dark-haired girl came inside and closed the door behind her. She was wearing a dark coat and tam but no gloves.

Mr. Tallant stood up. "Come in. Come in. What can we do for you?" He smiled at the girl as she slowly walked toward him.

"Ma said I had to go to school," the girl said when she finally reached Mr. Tallant's desk. She nervously pulled at the pocket of her coat.

"Did anyone come with you to enroll you in the school here?" Mr. Tallant asked.

"No, sir, Ma's not feeling well and told me to come on by myself," the girl said. She did not have the local accent.

"I'm sorry she's ill, but we can get you started," the schoolmaster assured her. Indicating a chair by his desk, he said, "Please sit down for a minute."

The girl sat down. "Now, what is your name, miss?" Mr. Tallant asked.

"Faith Winters, sir."

Mr. Tallant wrote on his tablet. "What year of school are you in?"

"I've been going to school for four years now," she replied.

"Where do you live?" Mr. Tallant asked.

"You go down this road and then go left, and about a half mile on, there's the house," Faith replied.

Mr. Tallant looked puzzled for a moment. Then he nodded. "Oh, you live in the house where Mr. Conley used to live."

"Yes, sir," Faith replied.

So this was who was living there! Mandie

couldn't wait to make friends with the girl and find out all about her. Seldom did a new friend move into the community. Charley Gap snuggled down between the mountains and was not a place that attracted outsiders. Everyone who lived around there knew everyone else, and their families had lived there forever.

"Now, I have my students divided into four groups, according to their ages, and there are four in each group. You will make five in one group," Mr. Tallant explained. He stood up, looked around the schoolroom, and focused on Mandie's section of the room. "Esther, will you please share your books with Faith today? I believe you are the only one with a double desk that is not being fully used."

Mandie was surprised to see Esther frown and to hear her mumble under her breath. Esther moved all her books onto her side of the desk.

Mr. Tallant walked with Faith to Esther's desk. "Faith, this is Esther," he said. "And, Esther, if you'll share your books with Faith today, I'll get some books down from the attic this afternoon for Faith."

Mandie noticed that Esther did not say a word. She glanced across the room and saw that Joe was listening and watching too.

As Faith started to sit down with her coat and tam on, Mr. Tallant pointed to the back. "You may hang your things on the pegs at the door."

Faith removed her coat and tam, hung them on the pegs, and came back to the desk. She wore an ill-fitting navy blue dress and acted as though she was cold, even though Mr. Tallant kept the room warm. Mandie decided Faith was awfully shy. Despite the other students' curious stares, she wouldn't look directly at anyone.

"This is Group Two, Faith," Mr. Tallant explained, standing by Esther's desk. "This group will read silently, Chapter Two, in your reading book. And I'll need to get a little more information from you later, Faith."

"Yes, sir," Faith said quietly.

Mandie planned to talk with Faith when recess came. But to her disappointment, Faith went to Mr. Tallant's desk at noontime. "You wanted to ask me more questions, you said, sir. I have to go home now. I can't stay all day today."

"Of course, Faith," Mr. Tallant said, picking up his pencil. "But you will be planning to stay all day after this, won't you?"

"Yes, sir," Faith said. "But today I have to go home and see about Ma."

"I understand," Mr. Tallant replied. "Sit down for a minute. This won't take long. I need to get some information about your previous school from you."

The other students had all grabbed their lunch baskets and gone outside, even though the weather was cold. Joe beckoned to Mandie, and she joined him on the porch.

"At least she doesn't look like an outlaw," Joe teased as they sat on the steps to eat their lunch.

Mandie smiled back. "I wonder whether her mother is bad sick. Your father could go call on her if she is, and we could find out all kinds of things."

"Oh, no, Mandie," Joe said, shaking his head. "Just because he's a doctor doesn't mean he can nose around in people's business."

"Well, I didn't exactly mean nose around," Mandie protested. "What I meant was, he would have to talk to her if she's sick and ask some questions."

"Like what?" Joe asked as he bit into his sausage biscuit.

"Like, where did they come from? Faith has a funny accent that I've never heard before," Mandie replied. She began eating her lunch. "I have a great idea," she said suddenly. "Next—"

"You always have great ideas," Joe interrupted. "You'd better finish your food. We have to go back inside in a minute."

"We should have eaten at our desks. Then we could have heard what Mr. Tallant was asking her," Mandie said, devouring the cookie in her lunch basket.

"You call that a great idea?" Joe asked in surprise.

"No, that's not what I was going to say," Mandie replied, taking a swallow of milk from the small jug in her basket. "What I was going to say was, next week is Thanksgiving. I could get my mother to let me cook something to take over to Faith and her mother. Then I would be able to get inside and meet her."

Other students were drifting back inside. Mandie closed her lunch basket and stood up. "Come on, let's go back to our desks."

Just as Mandie stepped through the schoolroom doorway, she came face to face with Faith. She'd put on her coat and tam.

"Hello, Faith," Mandie greeted the girl with a big smile.

Faith pretended she didn't hear and kept on going right out the door.

"Well," Mandie said in surprise as she removed her coat and bonnet and hung them up.

"I don't think she wants to be friends with anyone," Joe remarked as he hung his coat alongside Mandie's. He bent down to whisper in Mandie's ear, "Or she has a deep dark secret she doesn't want anyone to know about."

Mandie's blue eyes grew round as she looked up at Joe. "You're probably right!" she said. "That's why things are so mysterious over at her house. I'll investigate."

Mandie went on to her desk, thinking about what Joe had said. She knew he was only teasing, but maybe he had guessed the truth about Faith.

Why else would she seem so afraid? *I'll talk Mama into letting me bake something for Thanksgiving and take it over to Faith and her mother,* she thought excitedly.

As Joe said, she always had great ideas!

5

Holiday

MANDIE WALKED DOWN the aisle between her desk and Esther's. She smiled as she said, "Good morning, Faith." It was Friday, and Mandie was hoping to get to know Faith before the weekend.

But Faith ignored her and she continued to thumb through the books that Mr. Tallant had given her.

Mandie took a deep breath. "I'd like to be your friend, Faith."

Faith turned away from her without a word. At that moment Esther arrived. Esther put her books on her side of the double desk and flopped down. "Well, I suppose you're going to sit by me all the time."

Faith didn't say anything. Mandie was glad of

that. Clearly, Faith didn't want to make friends with anyone. It wasn't just Mandie.

Frustrated, Mandie went to her own desk. *Somehow* she was going to get to know Faith.

No one else spoke to Faith the rest of the day. To Mandie's dismay, the other girls were giggling behind Faith's back and making signals with their faces and hands. That made Mandie all the more determined to be Faith's friend.

At recess Mandie and Joe saw Faith slip through the crowd, evidently still wanting to be alone. Faith took her lunch basket, walked to the farthest tree, and sat down on a stump to eat.

"She won't even speak to me, Joe," Mandie complained as they sat on a bench near the front porch with their lunch.

"Give her time. After all, she had to walk into the schoolhouse all alone, into the middle of all those staring eyes," Joe replied.

"I'll just keep saying good morning to her every day until she finally speaks to me, I suppose," Mandie said, taking her biscuit out of its napkin. "You know, she has on the same dress she had on yesterday. She may not have many clothes."

"She probably doesn't, living in that old, tumbledown house," Joe said.

"Do you think that's what the other girls are giggling about?" Mandie asked, biting into her biscuit.

"I don't know, but I imagine Mr. Tallant will soon put a stop to all that," Joe replied, looking through his lunch basket.

"I hope he does," Mandie said.

When Monday came, the other girls were still giggling and acting silly. Mandie frowned as she watched Esther make a face at another girl across the room as she pointed to Faith's back. Faith had on the same dress again. Maybe the girls were making fun of her clothes. Mandie was itching to say something to the fun-makers, but she didn't dare in the schoolroom.

About an hour before school was to let out, Faith arose and began stacking her books. Mr. Tallant looked at her but instead of asking her why she was leaving, he nodded.

"See you in the morning, Faith," he said as Faith got her coat and tam.

"Yes, sir," Faith replied, hastily putting on her

coat and tam and picking up her books from the floor. She rushed out the door and closed it behind her.

About five minutes after that, Mr. Tallant tapped on his desk and stood up. "Attention, everyone," he said loudly. Sixteen pairs of eyes looked up from the books.

"I'm sorry I have to bring up the subject of misbehavior, but most of you have been very rude where it concerns our new student, Faith Winters. I have seen what's going on and I want you to know that I will not stand for it. From this moment on, anyone who is caught giggling, making signs, or talking about Faith behind her back will immediately be failed in deportment—and I don't believe your parents would like that. I'm sure they thought you had all been raised better. You should be ashamed of yourselves."

Mandie said a silent thank-you to Mr. Tallant.

"Now, get back to your books, but just remember what I have said," the schoolmaster continued. "I'm not asking that you befriend the girl if you don't want to, but I am asking that you not ridicule her. I'll be watching and listening tomorrow morning."

The next day Mandie and Joe arrived early. Faith was already at her desk. Mandie paused on the way to her desk to say, "Good morning, Faith." But Faith said nothing.

"I have some good news that I think all of you will like," the schoolmaster began, tapping on his desk. "School will close this afternoon for the Thanksgiving holiday and won't reopen until next Monday."

Mandie broke the silence as she called to him, "Thank you!" All the other students began to talk excitedly.

"Now let's calm down and get our work done," Mr. Tallant said, tapping on his desk once more. "And then I won't give you any homework for next Monday."

There was another roar of thank-yous, and then complete silence as everyone went back to their books.

When school let out, Mandie and Joe happened to be going out the front door at the same time Faith was. Mandie knew the girl had to walk the same way they did before she turned off on another road.

"Faith, want to walk with us? Joe and I go your way down to the first crossroad," Mandie said. But Faith slipped silently past them.

Mandie and Joe walked quickly to the road as Faith ran ahead of them.

"Might as well slow down. She's gone," Joe told Mandie when they reached the main road.

"I'll go to her house on Thanksgiving and bring something nice to eat," Mandie said. "Mama will be baking tomorrow. You know we are going to your house for Thanksgiving dinner, don't you?"

"Now, how could I not know that?" Joe teased as they walked on. "I've been hearing my mother planning the menu for a week."

"Are the McGoochins coming too?" Mandie asked.

"No, they don't like to bring Lucinda and Michael on such a long trip in bad weather, so they seldom come visit in the wintertime," Joe explained.

Mandie was pleased to hear that. Lucinda and Michael were not very friendly, and the clothes they wore always made Mandie feel poor. She was not comfortable around them.

That night Mandie told her parents about Faith Winters. Irene had finally come downstairs for supper, and they sat around the big table in the kitchen.

"There's a new girl in our school," Mandie began, laying down her fork.

Everyone looked at her. New people in the community were a surprise to them also.

"Where did she come from?" Irene asked, pausing with a forkful of mashed potatoes in mid-air.

"Does she live around here?" Mr. Shaw asked.

"I hadn't heard of anyone new moving hereabouts," Mrs. Shaw said.

"She lives in the old Conley house," Mandie explained. "She's tall and has dark hair and Mr. Tallant put her in my group. She's pretty. I don't know where she came from, but she has a different accent from ours."

"Didn't you ask her?" Irene asked.

"She doesn't talk to anybody. She seems to want to be left alone," Mandie explained. Turning to her mother, she said, "Mama, when we bake tomorrow could we please make an extra pumpkin pie, and I'll take it over to her for Thanksgiving?"

"An extra pie's no problem, but it's a long way from here to the old Conley place," Mrs. Shaw said.

Mr. Shaw spoke up. "I'll drive you over there in the wagon. When do you plan on taking this pie to her?"

"Since we are going to the Woodards' for Thanksgiving dinner, maybe I could take it to her before we go there," Mandie suggested.

"All right, you get ready early and we'll drive over there Thanksgiving morning, then come back and get your mother and Irene."

"Thank you, Daddy," Mandie said with a big smile.

Mrs. Shaw baked the next day, and as was her custom, she baked enough to last a while. Mandie was allowed to mix the ingredients for the pumpkin pie. It turned out perfectly and Mandie was proud of herself. She couldn't wait to deliver the pie to Faith.

Mandie was up bright and early Thanksgiving Day and helped her father cook breakfast. Mrs.

Shaw and Irene came into the kitchen when it was ready.

Windy too knew there was food. She jumped out of the woodbox and came to rub around Mandie's ankles as she set the table.

"No, Windy, you can't eat yet," Mandie said to the kitten, stooping. "You go sit by the stove while we eat. Then I'll give you what's left."

The kitten purred and continued following Mandie around the room.

"Why don't you give her some bacon rind? She can gnaw on that while we eat," Mr. Shaw said.

"That's a good idea," Mandie agreed, going to get the rind.

Mrs. Shaw had given permission for the kitten to stay in the house, but she still wasn't friendly with Windy. "Let's all sit down now," she said. "If you're going to take that pie to Faith you'll have to hurry."

"Yes, ma'am," Mandie said as the family sat down to breakfast.

As soon as the meal was finished, Mr. Shaw harnessed the horse to the wagon and he and

Mandie, who held the pie carefully in her lap, drove over to Faith's house.

Mr. Shaw had to stop the wagon on the road because the driveway was overgrown with weeds and bushes. "I'll wait right here while you go to the door," he told Mandie. "Let me hold the pie while you get down." He took the dish.

Mandie jumped down, reached back up for the pie, and hurried down a narrow trail to the front door of the house. She knocked loudly, waited a minute, then knocked again.

Finally the door opened a crack. Faith peered out.

"I brought you and your mother a pumpkin pie for Thanksgiving. I made it myself," Mandie explained with a big smile.

Before Faith could reply, Mandie heard a woman's voice inside the house. "Dear, who is it?"

Faith looked nervously over her shoulder. "A girl from school."

The woman called back, "Well, hurry and close the door, dear, before all the heat goes out."

Mandie held the pie out to Faith. "Please take it."

Faith grabbed the pie plate. "Thank you. Goodbye." To Mandie's surprise, she slammed the door.

Mandie went back to the wagon. "She was just plain rude, Daddy. She didn't even ask me in!"

"That's all right, dear. We're in a hurry anyway." He looked around the yard as the horse pulled the wagon on. "I wonder if Faith has a father or uncle or some male kin living here. The place sure could use some work."

Mandie thought for a moment. "No, I believe Faith told Mr. Tallant it was only her and her mother."

"If it's just the girl and her mother, I wonder what they do for a living," Mr. Shaw said thoughtfully.

Mandie looked up at her father sitting next to her. "I don't know, Daddy. They probably don't have much money."

"I tell you what. Why don't you and I round up some help and clean the place up for them?"

"Oh, Daddy, could we?" Mandie cried. "That would be nice, to help them."

"I'll speak to Dr. Woodard today and see what

he knows about these people and also what he thinks about my idea."

"Thank you, Daddy," Mandie said. "I want to help too."

They went on home, picked up Mrs. Shaw and Irene and the cake and pie they were taking, and drove on to the Woodards'.

When they arrived, everyone was gathered in the parlor, where the Woodards' huge fireplace had a fire roaring.

"I took a pie to Faith and she wouldn't let me in," Mandie said the minute she saw Joe. "And while he was waiting for me, Daddy noticed the yard and the house need some work done to them." She looked at her father across the room.

"That's right," Mr. Shaw said. "It seems there's only a young girl and her mother living in the old Conley place now, and it's in bad shape. Why don't we get the men together and go clean it all up?"

"Why, certainly, we'll round everyone up and see what can be done," Dr. Woodard replied. "If I have to be out making calls, I'll send Mr. Miller to help. What kind of tools do we need to take?"

The Woodards' hired help, Mr. and Mrs. Miller, lived in a cabin down by the creek on the Woodards' land. The Millers took care of anything that the Woodards didn't have time to do. Mrs. Miller cooked and cleaned the house. Mr. Miller was in charge of farming the land.

"Some of everything, I suppose," Mr. Shaw said. "It's practically a wilderness around the old house."

"When are we going to do this, Daddy?" Mandie asked from across the room.

"The sooner the better," Mr. Shaw replied.

"We can supply the food for whoever works," Mrs. Shaw said.

"I think if we could pass the word around today, most of the men hereabouts could start work tomorrow, and school is out, so the young ones could help too," Mr. Shaw said.

"I'll get Mr. Miller going on it as soon as we eat," Dr. Woodard agreed.

Mandie turned to Joe. "I'm going too. Are you?"

Joe looked doubtful. "Of course I'm going, but I don't know what you're going for. This is men's work."

"Joe Woodard, there are lots of things I can do: pick up garbage, sweep the yard, and all that," Mandie replied.

"I know why you're going. You think you can get inside the house," Joe teased her.

"I don't just think it," Mandie said. "I know I will. Somehow."

6

Everybody Pitches In

THE NEXT DAY WAS a little warmer than it had been, and the sun was shining. Mandie knew that once they got working on Faith's yard they would all warm up. Her mother didn't want her to go, but by promising to take care of the food Mrs. Shaw was sending for the workers, Mandie was finally allowed to accompany her father.

"I can serve the men at noon when they take a break to eat," Mandie promised her mother.

"Well, I suppose you could, but this is no job for a girl to be going on," her mother replied as she packed up pails of fried chicken, baked potatoes, and freshly baked biscuits.

Irene had come into the room. "I could help you, Mandie, couldn't I?"

Mandie shrugged. "I suppose so, if you really want to."

"Irene, you're just getting well again," Mrs. Shaw said. "I'm not so sure you ought to be out in the cold all day."

"I'll wrap up real good, Mama," Irene promised. "And I can always stay in our wagon under the cover. Please, Mama."

Mrs. Shaw finally agreed. "All right. But be sure you wear a scarf, a hat, and gloves. And don't come home with any more excuses of a cold in order to stay out of school, you hear?"

"Yes, Mama, I won't," Irene promised, hurrying into the other room to grab her things.

Mandie knew very well why her sister wanted to go. Irene never did any work that she could get out of. It was because Tommy Lester and his father were going to be there.

Mr. Shaw brought the wagon to the back door and loaded the food in it along with the tools he was taking. Mandie and Irene both jumped up on the seat with him, and they hurried off to meet the other workers in front of Faith's house. As it turned out, they were the first ones there.

Mr. Shaw pulled the wagon to a stop on the road in front of Faith's house. Mandie caught a glimpse of a woman dressed in black, with a black shawl around her head, rushing into the house and closing the door.

"Since you know the girl, Amanda, I think you'd better come with me to the door," Mr. Shaw said, getting down from the wagon and reaching up for Mandie's hand as she jumped down.

"Yes, sir," Mandie said.

"I'll wait here in the wagon and watch for the others," Irene told them.

Mandie and her father walked through the brambles to the front door, where Mr. Shaw knocked firmly. Faith opened the door and held it against her to keep them from seeing inside.

"Please go away," she said. "Ma is not well."

"Oh, but we don't need to see anyone. We have come to clean up your yard. All the other men in the community are coming along any minute too. We just wanted you to know what we're doing," Mr. Shaw explained as he smiled at her.

"No, please go away. Ma is not well," Faith insisted, holding firmly to the door.

"I'm sorry she's not well, but we won't bother y'all. We're just going to work here in the yard," Mr. Shaw told her again.

Several other wagons had arrived and were parking along the road. Mr. Shaw went out to meet them.

"Faith, we're only trying to help you. That's the way people in this community are. We help each other out when it's needed," Mandie tried to explain.

"Please go away," Faith said, and quickly closed the door.

Mandie went out into the yard to join Joe, who was with Mr. Miller.

"My father had to make some calls, so Mr. Miller came in his place," Joe was telling Mr. Shaw. "My mother sent lots of food. I suppose we'll just leave it in the wagon until everyone wants to eat."

"Thanks, Joe," Mr. Shaw said, and turned away to speak to some of the other men.

"We brought lots of food too," Mandie told Joe. "Now, what are you planning to do?"

"There are quite a few men out there. Why

don't you and I go into the yard and collect the garbage?" Joe suggested.

"What kind of garbage? And what are we going to do with it?" Mandie asked, looking around them.

"Any kind of garbage. We brought some croker sacks to put it in, and we can go dump it on their back property line until someone can haul it off somewhere," Joe explained, going back toward the Woodards' wagon. "I'll get the sacks."

The men were unloading their tools and fanning out over the property. Mandie knew they would cut the bushes, trim the trees, and pull out weeds. As Joe came back dragging a bunch of croker sacks, she pulled one of the burlap bags from the tangle. "I'll begin in the front yard."

"Then I'll do the back yard," Joe told her, putting the sacks by the front porch. "I'll leave the bags right here for you to take whenever you need another one. And when your bag gets full, holler and I'll come help you carry it to the back."

"All right," Mandie agreed. She began picking up old pieces of paper, cans, and other discarded items, and put them in her bag, which she dragged along with her as she went. Now and then she looked up to see if anyone had come out of the house, but there was no sign of anyone.

Before long she had a bag full of garbage. "I've got one full," she called to Joe.

"So have I! Wait and I'll come help you."

He came to meet her halfway, leaving his bag in the back yard.

"It's going to be a job carrying it through the back yard," Joe replied, stooping to grab an end of her bag.

Mandie got the other end, and they carried it down what had once been a trail to the barn. Now it was covered with brambles.

"Let me chop some of that stuff out of your way," Mandie's father called to them.

He came to meet them, and one of the other men came to help. The men went ahead and cleared the way toward the back of the property. Mandie and Joe followed with the bag. It was a slow process, but eventually the path was open far enough for Mandie and Joe to dump the garbage on what Mr. Shaw said must be the edge of the property. There was a creek flowing under the trees, and he cautioned them not to put it close to the water.

"We don't want to pollute the water, so be sure you don't dump anything any nearer than the top of the hill. We don't know when someone will be able to carry it off," he told them.

"Yes, sir," Joe said, pointing where Mr. Shaw had indicated. "We'll pile it all up here."

"We're going to have lots of it, Daddy," Mandie said. "This is just the first bag!"

On their way back to the yard, Mandie and Joe stopped by the barn and looked inside.

"Look! There's an old wagon!" Mandie said. She ran inside.

Joe followed and examined the vehicle. "And it looks like it could be repaired enough to use. I don't believe it's rotten, and the wheels look all right," he said, stooping to look under it.

"But, Joe, they don't have a horse. So what good is it?"

"I know!" Joe said suddenly. "My father has several old horses that are hardly ever used. They get old and he just buys younger ones and keeps on feeding the old ones. All they do is wander around the pasture. Maybe he would let Faith and her mother have one! I'll ask him. And I could help repair this wagon and get it rolling again."

"And I could get my father and the other men to furnish the feed," Mandie added.

As they walked back toward the house, they looked around the property.

"Joe, the fence will have to be repaired before you can put a horse in there, or it might run away," Mandie said, pointing to the missing sections of the rail fence.

"That's not a big job," Joe said.

They passed what had at one time been an enclosure for chickens and stopped to inspect it.

"And this fence for the chickens needs fixing too," Joe remarked.

"And the chicken coop is falling apart. Look," Mandie said, pointing to the small shed inside the broken-down fence.

"I don't believe they have any chickens. I don't see any," Joe told her, looking around.

Mandie smiled. "If you're going to see about the horse, then I'll see about the chickens. I know my mother would probably give them at least one chicken, and if all the other neighbors would give one each, why, they'd have a chicken coop full!"

"And we may have an extra rooster," Joe said.

"I'd like to get a peek inside the house." Mandie said as they walked back toward it. "I know all the women will help fix it up if we can just persuade Faith to let us."

Mandie and Joe worked on the yard until noontime, when Joe helped her set the food out in the back of their wagons. Irene and Tommy Lester had disappeared just as Mandie had predicted, but when the food came out they reappeared. While all the men sat on the ground eating, Mandie and Joe told them their ideas.

By the time almost all of the food had been eaten, Mandie had managed to get promises from all of them. A rooster and hens, and the feed for them, had been promised by Mr. Shaw. One neighbor had promised to donate eggs from his chickens. Several had volunteered to feed the horse that Joe thought his father would give.

"And since there's not a man here to help, we can all take turns checking on things and doing odd chores," Mr. Shaw said as he looked around at the men.

"Aye," they all agreed.

Mandie looked at Joe and smiled. "Look what we've accomplished," she whispered.

"I'm thankful we were able to," Joe said as everyone got back to work.

The men worked until the sun started to set; then Mr. Shaw called to Mandie and Joe that it was time to go home.

"I'll just go to the door and tell Faith that we'll come back tomorrow to do some more work," Mr. Shaw told the other men as they prepared to leave.

"Same time," several of the men called as they drove off.

Mandie followed her father to the front door and waited by the window. Joe had left with Mr. Miller.

"You may have to knock several times to get Faith to answer," Mandie told her father.

As he tapped on the door, Faith opened it a small crack and looked out.

"Just wanted to let you know we'll all be back

tomorrow about the same time to try and get more done," Mr. Shaw told her. "And then—"

"Please go away," Faith said, interrupting.

"Then next week we'll come over anytime we can and work on the barn and the fence," Mr. Shaw continued.

"I told you my ma isn't well," Faith insisted, quickly pushing the door shut.

At that moment Mandie glanced inside the window through a crack in the curtain, and held her breath in shock. There was a woman sitting with needlework of some kind in her lap. Her face was covered with scars! *The poor woman! What could have happened to her face?* Mandie couldn't stop peeking inside.

"Come on, Amanda, we're going home," Mr. Shaw told her.

Mandie quickly ran after him to the wagon. Irene was already there, waiting for them.

"Daddy!" Mandie exclaimed as she jumped up onto the seat. "There was a woman inside with an awful face!" She held her breath in horror.

Mr. Shaw started the wagon rolling. "What do you mean?"

"This woman was sitting by the window and I

saw her face," Mandie explained breathlessly. "It was horrible. Something must have happened to her!"

Mr. Shaw quickly glanced at her. "What do you mean, horrible?"

"Oh, Daddy, her face was covered with awful scars! I've never seen anything like it," Mandie said.

"The woman must be Faith's mother," Irene put in.

"Yes, she must be," Mr. Shaw said. "Are you sure her face was scarred, Amanda?"

"I'm sure, Daddy." She shivered and hugged herself. "Oh, she looked absolutely horrible."

"Maybe that's why Faith didn't want us around," Mr. Shaw said as they traveled down the road toward home.

"She kept saying her mother was not well," Mandie reminded him.

"And I heard her tell y'all to go away," Irene added.

"I wonder if the scars are new, or if it was something that happened a long time ago," Mr. Shaw said, pulling the wagon into their back yard.

"I don't know, Daddy, but I'm going to try to find out," Mandie said as she jumped down from the wagon.

Mrs. Shaw came to the door as the girls brought in the remains of the food they had taken for the noon meal. Mandie immediately began telling her mother about what had been going on, and about the woman with the scarred face.

"I'm sorry, Amanda, but how about getting cleaned up first, and then we'll talk? I need to put supper on the table," her mother told her.

Later, as the Shaw family discussed the woman Mandie had seen through the window, her mother had a suggestion. "Amanda, could you have mistaken shadows for scars? You said you couldn't see very well."

"Oh, no, Mama!" Mandie replied. "I clearly saw the woman's face, and it was scarred."

"I'm wondering about that too, Amanda," Mr. Shaw said. "Maybe your mother is right. There could have been shadows on the woman's face."

"That's right, Mandie," Irene put in.

"I know what I saw!" Mandie said, becoming irritated because no one seemed to believe her.

"Don't get upset, dear," her father said. "We're not saying you're wrong, but there's a possibility."

"No, no, no!" Mandie declared. "I saw scars! And I'll prove it to y'all."

"And how are you going to do that?" Irene asked.

"I—I—" Mandie sputtered. Finally, she said, "I don't know right now, but I'll figure out how to prove what I saw."

Mandie thought about the woman long after she had gone to bed that night. What had happened to the woman's face? Whatever it was, it must have been horrible. And that was probably why Faith had acted so strange.

It looked as if Mandie had another mystery to solve.

7

Secrets Uncovered

SATURDAY MORNING THE MEN returned to Faith's house to do more work. Mandie had a hard time convincing her mother to let her go.

"I don't think you ought to spend today there too," Mrs. Shaw told her in the kitchen after breakfast. "We have lots of work to do here."

"But, Mama, I want to go with Daddy," Mandie argued. "Besides, I've been doing all the work here every Saturday since Irene has been sick."

Mrs. Shaw looked at her a moment as she packed food for the men. "I suppose you're right," she said. "You have been doing a lot. You just go ahead, and Irene can stay and help me today. But, mind you, there will probably be things left to do after you get home this afternoon. I understand the men are not going to stay all day, just halfway into the afternoon."

"Thank you, Mama," Mandie said gratefully as she helped with the food. "I won't mind. Whatever you have for me to do when I get home, I'll be glad to do it."

Mr. Shaw had gone out to the barn to harness the horse to the wagon. Mandie looked through the window and saw him pulling the vehicle up to the back door.

"I have to get my coat. Daddy's out there," Mandie said, rushing into the front room. She quickly pulled on her coat and bonnet and stuffed her gloves in her pocket. *Another exciting day,* she thought as she raced back into the kitchen to help load the food into the wagon. Her mother had gone outside.

Irene had been upstairs but had come down into the kitchen. She glanced at the food. "So you are going over there again today?" she asked.

"Yes, Mama said I could," Mandie told her, picking up a heavy pail and starting for the back door.

"I don't know why you want to go there. I sure don't want to waste *my* time hanging around there again today," Irene said with a sniff.

Mandie stopped to look back at her sister. "I think it will be fun." Her blue eyes twinkled. "Don't work too hard today." Before Irene could blink, she rushed outside.

"What?" Irene called after her with her mouth wide open.

Mandie knew her sister had just realized that with Mandie gone, she would have to do all the work at home. She was sure her sister was not going to like it.

When Mr. Shaw pulled their wagon to a stop in front of Faith's house, Mandie jumped down and went to look for Joe. He was down by the barn, chopping firewood, and she was surprised to see Tommy Lester helping him.

"Good morning," Mandie greeted them. "What can I do to help?"

Joe stopped to take a breath. "I don't think you can chop wood."

"You're too little to swing the ax," Tommy added, grinning at her. "But you might be able to carry a log—a little log, that is—now and then to the back porch."

Mandie frowned. She wanted to contribute too. "Y'all are piling the wood on the back porch?" she asked Joe.

"Yes, until the porch gets full," Joe said. "Then we'll pile it under the porch so it will stay dry."

"All right, I can help do that," Mandie said. She bent to pick up a log that had been chopped small enough to go into the cookstove. "They're not so heavy."

"These for the stove are not, but later we'll chop wood for their fireplace. They'll be much bigger and heavier," Joe said, going back to his work.

Mandie began carrying the logs to the back porch, passing the well on the way. Now and then Joe stopped chopping to take an armful of wood with her. On one of her trips, Mandie straightened up after picking up a log and looked toward the house. Faith was coming out the back door with a bucket in her hand. She was heading straight to the well.

"Joe!" Mandie softly called to him. "Look!" She indicated Faith with her eyes.

Joe laid down the ax and hurried toward Faith. Mandie followed. Faith was already drawing water out of the well.

"Let me help you," he said, reaching for the rope that pulled the bucket up from the well.

"No, I know how to do this myself," Faith argued, catching the bucket full of water as it appeared at the top of the well.

"I know you do, but I'd like to help," Joe insisted, managing to slip the bucket out of Faith's hand.

Faith sighed. "Take it to the back porch, then, and set it down."

Joe didn't answer but hurried toward the back porch with the bucket. Instead of setting it down, he went on to the back door with it.

"Wait! No!" Faith cried, running after him. Mandie was right behind her. Before the girls could reach him, he entered the house.

Faith and Mandie burst into the kitchen behind Joe. The woman Mandie had seen through the window the day before was sitting by the cookstove with her back toward them.

"Hurry, Faith, dear, and close the door," the woman said.

"Go away," Faith said in an angry whisper to Joe and Mandie, motioning to the door.

Mandie and Joe didn't move. The woman turned to see Faith. When she saw Mandie and Joe standing there, she quickly pulled her black shawl over her head. But not before Mandie and Joe had both seen her scarred face.

"Mrs. Winters—" Mandie started.

"My name is not Winters," the woman interrupted.

Mandie looked questioningly at Faith. "She is Mrs. Chapman, my grandmother," the girl said, sounding upset.

"Your grandmother?" Mandie asked in surprise. She suddenly realized Faith called her grandmother Ma.

Faith looked her straight in the eyes, her own dark eyes blazing. "I don't have a mother or a father. Is there anything else you want to know?" She was practically screaming.

Mandie was shocked by Faith's behavior.

Joe pulled on Mandie's hand. "Come on, Mandie. Let's go," he said.

"I'm sorry," Mandie whispered as she and Joe went back out the door.

"I wonder what happened to her mother and father," Mandie said. She was shaken by Faith's attitude and the knowledge that she had no parents. "And what happened to her grandmother's face?" Tears filled her blue eyes as she followed Joe back to the woodpile.

Joe looked at her as he picked up his ax. "Why don't you sit down over there on that stump and rest awhile?"

Mandie remained standing. Her mind was spinning. "Joe, could your father do anything to make that poor lady's face better? Is there any way to remove all those scars?"

"No, my father isn't that kind of doctor," Joe replied, leaning on his ax. "But he might know a doctor who could help."

"Then I want to talk to your father," Mandie said. If anyone could help, Dr. Woodard could.

When it was time to pack up and go home, Mandie explained to her father about the woman.

"So she really does have a scarred face," Mr. Shaw said as he loaded his tools into the wagon.

"We'll take Joe home and see if we can catch his father."

When they got to the Woodards' house, Dr. Woodard was not there. Just as they were about to leave, the doctor came driving up in his buggy. Mandie and Joe ran up to him as he jumped down. Between the two of them they explained about the woman. Mr. Shaw stood by, listening.

"I would have to look at the woman's face to know whether anything might be done, and whether I could refer her to a doctor in that field," Dr. Woodard explained. He looked at Mr. Shaw. "Did you see her?"

"No, but from what these two said, she's in pretty bad shape," Mr. Shaw said. "And of course we have no idea as to how it happened."

"I would say it was caused by fire," Joe suggested.

Dr. Woodard sighed. "If her skin is severely burned, it will be difficult to help her. However, I will take a look at it."

"Oh, Dr. Woodard, that's going to be hard to do. She wouldn't even look at us, and she covered up her head with her shawl," Mandie said.

"Faith won't let anyone in the house," Joe added. "We practically forced our way in with the bucket of water."

"Faith might not act that way if you tell her you're a doctor," Mr. Shaw suggested.

"Now I know why Faith didn't want to let us in," Mandie said sadly.

"I wonder how the girl and her grandmother happened to come to live in that old house, anyway," Dr. Woodard said.

"Yes, and where did they come from? None of the men who've been working there with me knew they were even living there," Mr. Shaw remarked.

"Faith has a different accent from anyone I know. They must have come from way off somewhere," Mandie added. She thought of how quiet and sad-looking Faith had been at school. "Please, Dr. Woodard, you will go see her, won't you?" Mandie pleaded.

"Yes, of course. But I think maybe you'd better come with me, Miss Amanda," the doctor replied. "Faith knows you. Maybe you could persuade her to let us in the house." He turned to Mr. Shaw. "Suppose Joe and I meet you all at

Faith's house after we come home from church and have our dinner, say around two-thirty?"

"That would be fine," Mr. Shaw agreed.

Mandie was excited about the possibility of Dr. Woodard's helping Faith's grandmother. When she and her father got home, her mother and Irene were sitting in the kitchen by the cookstove, waiting for them. Mandie could smell the food cooking and saw that the table was already set for supper.

"Mama, I saw that woman's face up close. I was right—it is all scarred. But Dr. Woodard agreed to look at her," Mandie told her as she removed her coat and bonnet.

Mrs. Shaw cut her short. "You can tell us later. Now it's time to get cleaned up. Supper is ready."

"You saw the woman? Did she come outside?" Irene asked.

"No, Joe and I went into the house," Mandie explained.

"Amanda!" Mrs. Shaw said. "Get cleaned up."

"Yes, Mama," Mandie said.

Later, as they sat around the supper table,

Mandie told her mother and Irene about Mrs. Chapman and described her face. "And she's not Faith's mother. She's her grandmother," Mandie explained.

Mrs. Shaw put down her fork. "I wonder where these people came from."

"No one seems to know," Mr. Shaw replied.

"Maybe we can find out tomorrow when we go to see them," Mandie said. She felt Windy rubbing her ankles as she sat at the table, but she had to ignore her while they were eating. It was one thing for Mrs. Shaw to allow Windy in the house, but Mandie knew her mother would not like the kitten hanging around the table.

As soon as they were finished with their meal, Mandie gathered scraps from the table and put them in a bowl by the cookstove for Windy, who purred and began devouring the food.

Mandie thought about Faith. The girl didn't have a kitten or a sister—not even a mother. She must be awfully lonely with just her grandmother. *So why didn't she want to make friends with me?* Mandie wondered. Maybe if Dr. Woodard could find another doctor to fix Faith's grandmother's face, Faith would allow other people to come into the house and visit. Then Mandie heard what her father was saying to her mother.

"Those people seem to be awfully poor," Mr. Shaw was saying. "And the doctor Dr. Woodard is talking about probably lives a good distance from here. If Mrs. Chapman goes to consult with the other doctor, I don't know what will happen to the girl while she's gone."

"Maybe we could figure out something," Mrs. Shaw replied.

"Oh, Daddy," Mandie said, excitedly straightening up from petting Windy. "Could Faith come stay with us while her grandmother is gone?"

"Well, that would depend," Mr. Shaw said, picking up a book and sitting by the lamp.

"Yes. Faith's grandmother would have to decide what to do with Faith while she's gone," Mrs. Shaw agreed.

"Where would she sleep?" Irene asked.

"We could arrange something if it was necessary," Mrs. Shaw said.

"But just remember, nothing is definite right

now," Mr. Shaw said. "Dr. Woodard has to see Mrs. Chapman first. There may not be anything anyone can do."

Mandie wanted so much to help Faith and her grandmother. She knew Dr. Woodard would do his level best to find out if the woman's face could be fixed, but even if it could, would the woman agree to have anything done? An operation would probably be painful. She might not have the nerve to go through with it.

"But now that Faith knows we know about her grandmother, maybe Faith will be my friend," Mandie said quietly, nuzzling Windy's fluffy head. "There's nothing to hide anymore."

8

High Hopes

MANDIE SAT IMPATIENTLY through the Sunday-morning church service. Everything seemed to be moving awfully slowly. After church let out, her parents stopped to speak to almost everyone. When the Shaws finally got home, the noontime meal, although it had been cooked on Saturday as usual, had to be warmed and served. No one else seemed to be in a hurry as they sat around the table and ate.

But finally Mandie and her father were on their way to Faith's house. Dr. Woodard and Joe were waiting for them in their buggy.

"I think under the circumstances it will be better if you go up to the door and knock, Miss Amanda," Dr. Woodard told her as the four of them stood in the road. "The rest of us will be right behind you."

"Yes, sir," Mandie replied. She hurried up to the door and knocked loudly. She knocked again and again, until at last Faith opened the door a crack.

"What are you here for now?" she asked Mandie, wisps of her long hair framing her face.

"We would like to talk to your grandmother," Mandie told her.

Faith stuck her head out far enough to see that Dr. Woodard, Mr. Shaw, and Joe were standing on the porch. "What for?" she asked angrily. "So you can stare at her poor face?"

Before Mandie could reply, she heard Mrs. Chapman call out sternly, "Faith!"

Mandie quickly called to the woman, whom she couldn't see, "Mrs. Chapman, we have Dr. Woodard with us. He would like to talk to you to see if he can help you."

"I don't need any help, thank you," Mrs. Chapman answered.

Dr. Woodard reached forward and pushed the door open before Faith was aware of what he was doing. He stepped inside. "Mrs. Chapman, there may be a possibility that another doctor I know could do something about your face," he said, walking into the room toward the woman, who was seated by the warm cookstove. "If you would just allow me to ask you a few questions, I—"

Mrs. Chapman stood up, laying down the needlework she had been holding. She threw her shawl off her head and turned to face Dr. Woodard in the sunlight streaming through the window. "Ask what you like, but I've been told nothing can be done, so why waste your time and mine too?"

Dr. Woodard walked toward the woman, holding his hand out. "I'm the local doctor, Mrs. Chapman. I don't believe we've met."

"That's because we've only been here a few weeks," Mrs. Chapman said quietly."

Mr. Shaw joined the doctor. "I'm Jim Shaw, Mrs. Chapman, and we're probably your nearest neighbors. This is my daughter Amanda, and Dr. Woodard's son, Joe, both of whom are in school with your granddaughter."

"Would you mind telling me how this happened, Mrs. Chapman?" Dr. Woodard asked as he bent closer to examine her face.

Faith, who was standing near her grandmother, cried out, "It was all my fault! I set the fire!"

Mrs. Chapman reached out to touch her, but Faith ran across the room. "Dear, I've told you time and again it was not your fault that lamp exploded," Mrs. Chapman said, her voice heavy with emotion.

"Yes, yes, it was! *I* was the one who lit it. If I had stayed in the room to see that it was burning all right, I would have caught it before it blew up," Faith screamed. "Oh, my mother, my father!" She ran crying from the room.

"The poor child is not to blame," Mrs. Chapman told them with tears in her eyes. "She lit the lamp in the parlor and went upstairs to get the scarf she was working on. Before she could return, the lamp blew up and set the house on fire. She won't stop blaming herself. I just don't know what to do."

"Did you put the fire out? Is that how your face was injured?" Dr. Woodard asked.

"Everyone was upstairs, and the fire had spread by the time I smelled it," Mrs. Chapman explained. "Faith managed to escape through her bedroom window onto the roof of the front porch, but my poor daughter and her husband were trapped upstairs in another room. I tried to save them, but the old house was huge. It went up like kindling." She wiped her eyes with her shawl.

"Where were you living?" Mr. Shaw asked.

"St. Louis, and that's a big place," Mrs. Chapman replied. "No doctor there could do anything for me."

"Have you sought medical help from any doctors in New York?" Dr. Woodard asked.

"No, I've never been to New York," Mrs. Chapman replied. "It's so far away."

"I know a doctor there who, I think, may be able to help you," Dr. Woodard told her.

Mrs. Chapman shook her head. "That's impossible. I have to be frank with you so you'll understand. We lost everything in the fire. If it hadn't been for my cousin's willing us this place, we wouldn't have anywhere to stay."

"Was Mr. Conley your cousin?" Dr. Woodard asked.

"Why, yes, Al Conley was my only living relative besides my daughter. He came to live with us when he got too old to live alone," Mrs. Chapman said. "He passed away a few weeks before the fire."

"I knew Mr. Conley," Dr. Woodard told her. "I'm glad you gave him a home. He was too old and in too poor health to live alone." He paused to clear his throat. "Now, let's make arrangements for you to go to New York."

Mrs. Chapman quickly shook her head. "I can't afford it and don't have time to take away from my work to go."

"Your work?" Dr. Woodard asked.

"Yes, sir," the woman said. She picked up the needlework she had thrown down when they came in. She held it up for him to see. It was a pillowcase, and she was in the midst of attaching a wide row of tatting to the hem.

Mandie gasped in delight. "Oh, how pretty!" she exclaimed. "I wish I could do that."

Mrs. Chapman looked at her and smiled. "You could learn. Faith knows how to tat and helps me a lot. This is the way we make our living now," she explained.

Mr. Shaw reached out to touch the fabric.

"You don't say! You are very gifted. Who do you do this work for?"

"Different people," Mrs. Chapman said. "I do something for someone, and they show their friends, and then their friends ask me to do something for them. We have more orders than we can take care of. It doesn't amount to a whole lot of money, but we survive." She laid the pillowcase back on her chair. "That's the only kind of work I can do now, without going out in public."

"Have you done other work, Mrs. Chapman?" Mr. Shaw asked.

"Yes, I was a schoolteacher before this happened, but you see I had to quit," Mrs. Chapman replied, pushing her dark hair forward around her face. "Now, if y'all don't mind, I need to get this pillowcase finished before dark. I don't see too well at night anymore."

Mandie looked from Dr. Woodard to her father to Joe. They all seemed to be at a loss for words.

"Will you promise me that you will at least think about the possibility of going to New York?" Dr. Woodard asked.

"And if you're worried about the expense of the trip, I'm sure you have enough neighbors who will pitch in and help out with the money needed," Mr. Shaw told her.

Mrs. Chapman sighed. "I'll think about it, but that's all I can do right now."

Mandie and Joe followed their fathers out to the road to go home. Dr. Woodard and Mr. Shaw stood there a few minutes, talking.

"We need to figure out what we can do to help," Mandie said to Joe.

"That's exactly what I've been thinking, but I haven't been able to come up with any ideas," Joe answered.

"If we could learn how to tat, we could do some of her work for her while she's gone to New York," Mandie said.

Joe laughed. "Tat? Leave me out of that," he said with a big grin.

Mandie kicked the ground. "We'll just have to figure out something," she told him.

And by the next morning Mandie had figured out something! As she and Joe walked to school, she told him, "I've come up with a great idea! Miss Abigail probably knows how to tat. She could teach me and some other people and we could do Mrs. Chapman's work while she's away. Will you go with me to Miss Abigail's house after school today?"

Joe shrugged his thin shoulders. "All right, but I don't know what good it will do."

Miss Abigail didn't live very far from the schoolhouse. Mandie and Joe hurried there as soon as the bell had rung. Faith had not been at school that day, and Mandie figured she was still upset by what had happened the day before. Mandie wanted so much to do something for the girl. Maybe Miss Abigail had some ideas. And when Mandie had told Miss Abigail about Faith and her grandmother, Miss Abigail *did* know how to help.

"I happen to know how to tat, and I *could* teach you and some of the other neighbors. We could turn out more work for Mrs. Chapman while she's gone than she could do herself," Miss Abigail said as the three of them sat in her fancy parlor.

"Oh, thank you, Miss Abigail!" Mandie exclaimed. "Now we just have to talk Mrs. Chapman into going to New York."

"My father needs to go up there on some business himself and will take her," Joe said.

"Oh, Joe!" Mandie replied with joy. "What wonderful news!"

Miss Abigail smoothed her fluffy, snow-white hair and smiled at them. She was not old, but her hair had turned color prematurely. Her blue eyes sparkled as she joined in Mandie's plans.

"Do y'all think I should go and talk with Mrs. Chapman about this?" Miss Abigail asked.

"It might help," Mandie responded.

"I'll try," Miss Abigail promised.

"I asked my parents if Faith could stay with us while her grandmother is in New York, but they said they would see about it later," Mandie said.

"Oh, no," Miss Abigail said. "I insist that Faith stay here with me while her grandmother is gone. I have plenty of room. And it would be nice to have company for a while."

Mandie frowned. "You may have a problem with Faith. She blames herself for the fire. She doesn't want anything to do with anyone."

"That's too bad," Miss Abigail said. "But I think I can handle that. The main problem is getting Mrs. Chapman to agree to go to New York, isn't it?"

"Yes, ma'am," Mandie replied.

"I'll go over and talk to her this afternoon," Miss Abigail said.

That evening Mandie told her mother and father about her visit with Joe to Miss Abigail and about the promises the lady had made.

"It's good of Miss Abigail to try to help out," Mrs. Shaw said.

"I hope she will have some influence with Mrs. Chapman," Mr. Shaw said. "You may go by her house on the way home from school tomorrow and see what she has to say—that is, if Joe is able to go with you."

"Oh, thank you, Daddy," Mandie said.

But the next afternoon when the two young people called on Miss Abigail, they found that she had not been able to accomplish anything with Mrs. Chapman. Mrs. Chapman herself had answered the door, saying Faith was not feeling well and was upstairs.

"Mrs. Chapman told me the same thing she told you—Faith blames herself for the fire," Miss

Abigail said as they sat in her parlor. "I explained that we could take care of her business and Faith could stay with me while she is gone, but she said she couldn't go." Miss Abigail's expression was grim. "She says she doesn't have the time or the money, and that she can't go off and leave Faith."

Mandie was disappointed by Miss Abigail's news. "We'll just have to think up some way to work this all out," she told Miss Abigail.

"You're right," the lady replied. "You two think about it, and I'll try to come up with something."

The next afternoon Mandie and Joe walked over to Faith's house. They were surprised when Mrs. Chapman opened the door in answer to their first knock.

"Come in," she invited them. Her shawl was wrapped around her head and her hair hid part of her face.

"Mrs. Chapman, we want to help you go to New York to see that doctor," Mandie began.

"No, dear, forget about all that," Mrs. Chapman said, picking up her needlework. "I cannot go—no use talking about it."

"I was thinking, Mrs. Chapman, about the way Faith has been acting since we met you. Maybe if you would let a doctor help your face, Faith would quit blaming herself for it," Mandie said in a rush, trying to explain without hurting the lady's feelings.

"And my father is going to New York on business, so you could go with him," Joe added. "And Miss Abigail can take care of Faith and your work."

"I don't think having my face worked on would help Faith to forget what happened. No, Faith is more important to me than my face. There's no way I could go off and leave her here with Miss Abigail—or anyone else, for that matter," Mrs. Chapman replied with a worried frown.

"Don't you even want to see this doctor in New York and find out if he can help you?" Joe asked. "My father said it would be easier to do something now than wait until later, when the scars get old and set in place," he continued gently.

With shaking hands, Mrs. Chapman touched her face. "I can't leave Faith, so we might as well forget about all this." She bent over the needle-work in her lap. "Now, I've got work to do."

Mandie and Joe started for the door.

"I'm sorry, Mrs. Chapman," Mandie said.

"I'll explain to my father that you can't go with him," Joe added glumly.

Just as Joe reached to open the door, Faith came running into the room.

"Wait! Don't go! Wait!" she told Mandie and Joe as she knelt in front of her grandmother.

"Ma, you don't have to stay here with me," she burst out. "I want you to go to New York. I want you to see that doctor and see if he can fix your face. Please say you'll go."

Mrs. Chapman laid down her needlework and reached for Faith's hands. "You know I can't go off and leave you here," she told her, her voice choked.

"I'll be all right," Faith said. "I'll stay with Miss Abigail. I heard what she said when she came to visit you. You go on to New York with Dr. Woodard. I want you to."

Mrs. Chapman looked down at her. "Do you think you would be all right if I did go?"

"Of course, Ma! Of course. I've just realized

how selfish and mean I've been, thinking only of myself, when it's you who needs help. Please say you'll go. I don't want Joe to tell his father you aren't going. He'll go off and leave you, and you'll never have another chance to see that doctor in New York," Faith pleaded. "Please, Ma!"

Mrs. Chapman put her arms around Faith. "All right, all right, if you really want me to go, I'll go."

Mandie felt a thrill like a bolt of lightning run all over her. Tears came into her eyes as she looked at Joe and whispered, "We won, we won!"

"Yes," Joe whispered back.

"Is it all right if we go by Miss Abigail's house and tell her you're coming to stay with her, Faith?" Mandie asked.

Faith stood up and smiled at Mandie for the first time. She had a beautiful smile. "Sure, go ahead. And when Ma gets ready to leave, you and Joe could come back and help me take whatever things I'll be needing over to Miss Abigail's."

"We will," Mandie promised. "We have to go now, but we'll be back soon."

Mandie was so excited, her legs could hardly carry her out the door. Mrs. Chapman was going to New York to see that doctor and maybe get her face tended to, and Faith was going to stay with Miss Abigail. And almost best of all, Mandie knew Faith was going to be friends with her now. Everything had worked out wonderfully!

Whenever Mandie's around, a mystery is sure to follow. Find out what happens when one of Miss Abigail's most treasured objects disappears in *The Mystery at Miss Abigail's*.

Friendship Bank

Now that Mandie and Faith are friends, they enjoy writing special notes of encouragement to each other. Mandie saves the notes in an old coffee tin, and whenever she's feeling blue, she pulls one out and reads it. You and your friend can do this too!

Materials you and your friend will each need:
coffee can—rectangular or round
spray paint
old newspaper
stickers
scissors
small pieces of paper
a pen or pencil

1. Put your coffee can on the newspaper. Make sure the can is clean and dry, and that any paper labels are removed. Ask an adult to spray the can in the color of your choice. You probably will want to do this outside, or, if it's cold, in a garage or basement.

2. Cut a slit in the top of the lid. The slit should be between two and three inches long, and no more than one inch in width. Cutting the plastic is tricky, so make sure to ask an adult to help you.

3. When the can is dry, decorate it on all sides with stickers. You can spell out your name on the side if you like. Don't forget to decorate the lid! Place the lid on your friendship bank.

4. You're all set! Now, write your friend a note and have her write you one. After you read your friend's note, put it in your friendship bank. If you write to each other every day, your bank will soon be full. Each time you read the notes, you'll be reminded of your special friend . . . and how special you are, too!

About the Author

LOIS GLADYS LEPPARD has written many novels for young people about Mandie Shaw. She often uses the stories of her mother's childhood in western North Carolina as an inspiration in her writing. Lois Gladys Leppard lives in South Carolina.

The Mystery at Miss Abigail's

Mandie Shaw loves to visit her new friend, Faith, at Miss Abigail's big house. There they can play with each other and admire all the beautiful things. One thing the girls can't touch is the china cabinet in the front hall. It's full of precious china that only Miss Abigail is allowed to handle.

But when a beloved teapot turns up missing, does it mean a thief has broken into Miss Abigail's house? Will Miss Abigail have to tell the people of Charley Gap that they should lock their doors?

Mandie's determined to find the answer—and the missing teapot—in time for Miss Abigail's big Christmas party.

Coming in October 1999!